# This Makes Me Scared

Courtney Carbone

Illustrated by Hilli Kushnir

To Eric, for diving into this adventure with me —C.C.

To Liam and Aya, my team of bandits and partners-in-crime —H.K.

Text copyright © 2019 by Courtney Carbone
Cover art and interior illustrations copyright © 2019 by Hilli Kushnir

All rights reserved. Published in the United States by Rodale Kids,
an imprint of Random House Children's Books, a division of Penguin Random House LLC, New York.

Rodale and the colophon are registered trademarks of Penguin Random House LLC.

Visit us on the Web! rhcbooks.com

Educators and librarians, for a variety of teaching tools, visit us at RHTeachersLibrarians.com

Library of Congress Cataloging-in-Publication Data is available upon request.
LCCN 2018011831 (print) | LCCN 2018018246 (ebook) | ISBN 978-1-63565-081-5 (trade) | ISBN 978-1-63565-080-8 (pbk.) |
ISBN 978-1-63565-079-2 (ebook)

MANUFACTURED IN CHINA    10 9 8 7 6 5 4 3 2 1    First Edition

Random House Children's Books supports the First Amendment and celebrates the right to read.

RODALE KiDS

My swim class
begins today.

I am not sure
that I am ready.

3

The water looks deep.
I cannot see the bottom.

My body is shaking.

A whistle blows.
It is time to begin.

My heart is racing.
*Thump, thump, thump!*

My teacher shows me
how to float.

I try to float.
But I sink instead.

I start to panic.
Water goes up my nose.
I cough and sputter.

I reach for the wall
and hold on tight.

I climb a ladder
out of the pool.

My teacher follows.
She gives me a towel.

She asks me
how I am feeling.

My body is shaking.
My heart is racing.

What am I feeling?
I am feeling *scared*.

My teacher says
it is okay to be scared.

She says we can
face my fear together.

We practice
breathing deeply.

The air goes in and out.
We slowly count to ten.

My mind and body
start to calm down.

I am still scared.
But I am in control.

I am ready to try again.
I get back in the water.
My teacher holds
my hands.

I lie on my back.
I close my eyes.
My teacher slowly
lets go of my hands.

I pretend I am a cloud.
My whole body relaxes.

Soon I am floating!

I did it!
I faced my fear.

I am learning to swim.
Hooray!

I was very scared
at times today.
What makes YOU scared?